The Family Tree

Written by Oakley Graham
Illustrated by P.S. Brooks

TOP THAT

Licensed exclusively to Top That Publishing Ltd
Tide Mill Way, Woodbridge, Suffolk, IP12 1AP, UK
www.topthatpublishing.com
Copyright © 2017 Tide Mill Media
All rights reserved
2 4 6 8 9 7 5 3 1
Manufactured in China

ISBN 978-1-78700-218-0

A catalogue record for this book is available from the British Library

For my family with love - OG

A small tree stood alone on a grassy hill.

The seasons changed and the tree
was sad and lonely as it grew.

Then one day after many years of growing,
something amazing happened ...

A big tree stood on a grassy hill,
but it was no longer alone ...

It was a family tree.